Shirley
CHISHOLM

BY J. P. MILLER

ILLUSTRATED BY MARKIA JENAI

Rourke
Educational Media

A Division of
Carson Dellosa
Education

BEFORE AND DURING READING ACTIVITIES

Before Reading: *Building Background Knowledge and Vocabulary*

Building background knowledge can help children process new information and build upon what they already know. Before reading a book, it is important to tap into what children already know about the topic. This will help them develop their vocabulary and increase their reading comprehension.

Questions and Activities to Build Background Knowledge:

1. Look at the front cover of the book and read the title. What do you think this book will be about?
2. What do you already know about this topic?
3. Take a book walk and skim the pages. Look at the table of contents, photographs, captions, and bold words. Did these text features give you any information or predictions about what you will read in this book?

Vocabulary: *Vocabulary Is Key to Reading Comprehension*

Use the following directions to prompt a conversation about each word.

- Read the vocabulary words.
- What comes to mind when you see each word?
- What do you think each word means?

> **Vocabulary Words:**
> - *candidate*
> - *Congressperson*
> - *debate*
> - *election*
> - *political party*
> - *politics*
> - *slogan*
> - *terms*

During Reading: *Reading for Meaning and Understanding*

To achieve deep comprehension of a book, children are encouraged to use close reading strategies. During reading, it is important to have children stop and make connections. These connections result in deeper analysis and understanding of a book.

 Close Reading a Text

During reading, have children stop and talk about the following:

- Any confusing parts
- Any unknown words
- Text to text, text to self, text to world connections
- The main idea in each chapter or heading

Encourage children to use context clues to determine the meaning of any unknown words. These strategies will help children learn to analyze the text more thoroughly as they read.

When you are finished reading this book, turn to the next-to-last page for **Text-Dependent Questions** and an **Extension Activity**.

TABLE OF CONTENTS

RUNNING FOR PRESIDENT

Have you ever wanted to change the rules to make things fair? Have you ever dreamed of being someone who makes the laws? What about being president? Shirley Chisholm had those dreams. She was a leader in government. She was also a leader in staying true to what you know is right.

In the winter of 1972, people cheered when Shirley walked onto a stage. She announced that she wanted to be president of the United States. First, she would try to get her **political party** to vote for her as their choice for president. She wanted people to trust her to do the right thing. She was the first woman from the Democratic Party to try to be president. She was the first black **candidate** for president from any major party. She was ready to make a lot of changes.

Shirley was already a **Congressperson** from the state of New York. Shirley was black and proud, but she was just as proud to be a woman. She worked to make things fair for all kinds of people. Unlike some candidates, Shirley had not been given lots of money. Powerful people had not decided to help her. Shirley fought alone. Her plan was to "bring U.S."—us—"together."

FIGHTING SHIRLEY

Shirley was born in Brooklyn, New York. She moved with her three younger sisters to the country of Barbados when she was five years old. Her new school had many rules. It taught Shirley how to work hard. By the time she moved back to the United States when she was 10, she already knew that she was a strong person.

Shirley wanted to keep learning. She went to college and studied education. She worked in a school while she was a student. Once she finished college, she kept working in education. That was where she got interested in **politics**. How could she make education better for children? How could she help families?

She decided to work for the government. She could make changes happen there. In 1965, she won an **election**. She became a lawmaker for the state of New York. In just a couple of years, she made important steps toward her goal of improving people's lives.

Making Things Fair

Shirley started working right away in the New York state government. She was against a test that required people to use English to show that they could read. She thought that it was unfair to people who learned another language first.

Shirley decided to run for Congress. In 1968, she became the first black U.S. congressperson. Now, she would help make laws for the entire country.

Shirley went to Washington, DC. She would not allow anyone there to overlook her or tell her what to do. The first job she was offered was to be part of a group that helped make laws about farming. Shirley was upset. She wanted to improve education, not talk about farms. Shirley politely refused the job. She got the nickname "Fighting Shirley" because she was ready to fight to help people.

Shirley worked in Congress for seven **terms**. Because of her, it became against the law to pay maids, drivers, and nannies less than a certain amount. She helped start a program that gave food to women, babies, and children. This helped make sure that families could afford food even if they did not make a lot of money.

Shirley's hard work was making a difference in Congress. She wanted to help even more people. She decided to run for president of the United States.

A Powerful Office
In the 1960s and 1970s, women were not usually hired in politics. Shirley hired all women to work in her office. Half of her employees were black women.

Some people did not like what Shirley was doing or who she was. She got threats from people. She was treated unfairly. People tried to stop her from being on television. But Fighting Shirley was not going to give up.

She **gave speeches,**
...looked for solutions,
...and kept fighting!

Shirley worked hard in her fight to become president. Her **slogan** said a lot about her. It was on buttons and posters: "Vote Chisholm 1972, Unbought and Unbossed." No one could make her change her mind by giving her money. No one could tell her what to do. Nothing stopped Shirley from being who she was. In the end, she did not become president. But she changed the country just by being herself.

LEAVING A LEGACY

Shirley was a leader in many things. She was the first black woman in the U.S. Congress. She was the first black candidate from a major party to run for president of the United States. And she was the first woman to appear in a presidential **debate**.

Shirley did great things. But they were not why she wanted to be remembered. She wanted to be remembered for her strength. She wanted to be known as a woman who fought for change.

In 1983, Shirley retired from politics. She died in 2005 at the age of 80. Ten years after she died, she was honored for her work. President Barack Obama gave her the Presidential Medal of Honor. She had shown many people how to be an honest and strong leader.

"One does not learn, nor does one assist in the struggle, by standing on the sidelines..."
—Shirley Chisholm

TIME LINE

1924 Shirley is born on November 30th as Shirley Saint Hill in Brooklyn, New York.

1927–1934 Shirley lives in Barbados with her grandmother and sisters.

1946 Shirley graduates from Brooklyn College with a Bachelor of Arts degree.

1949 She marries Conrad Chisholm.

1952 Shirley earns a master's degree from Columbia University Teachers College.

1953–1959 Shirley becomes the director of the Hamilton-Madison Child Care Center.

1964–1968 Shirley is elected to the New York State Legislature. She serves as a Democratic member of the New York State Assembly.

1968 Shirley becomes the first African American woman elected to Congress. She represents New York's 12th District.

1969 Shirley becomes a founding member of the Congressional Black Caucus. She is the only woman among the founding members.

1970 Shirley becomes the cofounder of the National Organization for Women (NOW).

1970 Shirley publishes her book *Unbought and Unbossed* about her life.

1972 Shirley becomes the first African American person to run for president of the United States.

1972 Shirley tries to get the Democratic Party's presidential nomination. She does not win, but 151 officials vote for her.

1983 Shirley retires from politics.

1993 Shirley is nominated to be U.S. ambassador to Jamaica by President Bill Clinton, but withdraws.

2005 Shirley dies on January 1st.

2014 The U.S. Post Office releases a stamp in Shirley's honor.

2015 President Barack Obama honors Shirley with the Presidential Medal of Freedom.

2019 Shirley Chisholm State Park is opened in Brooklyn, New York.

GLOSSARY

candidate (KAN-di-date): a person who is applying for a job or running in an election

Congressperson (KAHNG-gris PUR-suhn): a person who is part of the lawmaking body of the United States, made up of the Senate and the House of Representatives

debate (di-BATE): a discussion in which people express different opinions

election (i-LEK-shuhn): the act or process of choosing someone or deciding something by voting

political party (puh-LIT-i-kuhl PAHR-tee): an organized group of people with similar political beliefs who sponsor candidates in elections

politics (PAH-li-tiks): the activity and discussions involved in governing a country, state, or city

slogan (SLOH-guhn): a phrase or motto used by a business, a group, or an individual to express a goal or belief

terms (turms): definite or limited periods of time, such as Congress's terms of two years, after which an official needs to be elected again

INDEX

TEXT-DEPENDENT QUESTIONS

1. What political office did Shirley Chisholm run for in 1972?

2. What was one thing that Shirley Chisholm did as a lawmaker in New York?

3. What was the first job Shirley Chisholm was offered in Congress?

4. How did Shirley Chisholm get the nickname "Fighting Shirley"?

5. What was Shirley Chisholm's presidential campaign slogan?

EXTENSION ACTIVITY

Imagine you are going to campaign to become president of the United States. Decide what things you want to do as president. Make a list of three things that will be important to you in your campaign. Write a speech explaining what you will do as president. Give your speech to a group of friends.

ABOUT THE AUTHOR

J. P. Miller is a debut author in children's picture books. She is eager to write stories about little- and well-known African American leaders. She hopes that her stories will augment the classroom experience, educate, and inspire readers. J. P. lives in Metro Atlanta, Georgia, and enjoys playing pickleball and swimming in her spare time.

ABOUT THE ILLUSTRATOR

Markia Jenai was raised in Detroit during rough times, but she found adventure through art and storytelling. She grew up listening to old stories of her family members, which gave her an interest in history. Drawing was her way of exploring the world through imagination.

www.rourkeeducationalmedia.com

Quote source: Shirley Chisholm, "The Black Woman in Contemporary America," speech, June 17, 1974, University of Missouri.

Edited by: Tracie Santos
Illustrations by: Markia Jenai
Cover and interior layout by: Rhea Magaro-Wallace

Library of Congress PCN Data

Shirley Chisholm / J. P. Miller
(Leaders Like Us)
ISBN 978-1-73163-803-8 (hard cover)
ISBN 978-1-73163-880-9 (soft cover)
ISBN 978-1-73163-957-8 (e-Book)
ISBN 978-1-73164-034-5 (ePub)
Library of Congress Control Number: 2020930058

Rourke Educational Media
Printed in the United States of America
01-1942011937